How the World Died: Some Alternative Views

David Macpherson

How the World Died: Some Alternative Views

1

Getting Into the Story

The old man stood on the gray beach, with his long unwieldy hair and his long white beard blowing in the wind like thin branches on a dead tree. He checked the closet crab trap and pulled with his old muscles and found three small green crabs. He tossed two of them in his rough hewn bag and he cracked the shell of the third with his tough fingers. The crab's eyes jumped forward and t hen expired until it was nothing but a platter for food. He Peeled off the shell and ate the meat raw. "Sashimi," he said, though he was not certain that he was giving the right description for what he was eating. It had been so long since he was a young man, attempting to impress a young woman at a mall court sushi bar. Or was that not even him but someone he watched in a movie or TV commercial eating such overpriced delicacies? Who knows. All he was sure of that the crabs now tasted different, like burnt licorice.

The dying crabs squirmed in the bag and the old man smiled. He stopped his little feast and looked around. He breathed in deeply and laughed. "Young bucks," he shouted. Nothing responded to him, "Young bucks. I smell you. Years in this blasted wasteland that was once a thriving civilization has allowed me to be able to smell unbathed neophyte hunters attempting to sneak up on me."

There was no sound for a few moments and then a voice behind a brush said, "What's a neophyte? That's not a word."

The old man laughed. That was his grandson, One Ear. He was always easy to suss out by using the words of the gone time. "Neophyte is what you are for if you were a seasoned hunter, you would not have fallen for my little ruse."

The bush shouted out again, "What's ruse?"

Another brush on the side of the beach shouted out, "Darn tarnation One Ear. Can't you be quiet for once and let us sneak up on the Grayling?

A third bush spoke up again, "Yes, how are we to be great hunter gatherers if we are not even to sneak up and kill a Grayling and to do that you need to shut up for once."

The first bush spoke quickly, "Were we really going to kill the Grayling. He is our grandfather and he usually has candy that he gives us."

"That candy is gross and no one should eat it. That candy is from the time before all this and our fathers have told us to never eat the candy the old gives us."

The third bush agreed, "That is the fourth law of the People of the Winnebago."

And all at once the three emaciated boys stood up and recited the Six Laws of the People of the Winnebago.

"Law one. We always share food we hunter gather.

"Law two. The people always bathe and keep clean but we never bathe more than once a month. More bathing that that is wasteful and weird.

"Law three. If the world below is rocking then don't go knocking."

The recitation ceased with One Ear interrupting, 'Can I just say I never understand that rule. Why would we knock on an earthquake?"

His cousin, Loopy," spat, "There are many interpretations explaining that but mostly you just have to follow the laws and not understand them. Can't you figure that out?"

"Law four, accept the candy from elders, but never eat it."

Law five, if you kill, make sure you don't know the name of the person you slay."

"Law six, marriage is forever unless you are totally sick of the whole thing."

The boys looked at one another and nodded, pleased that they recited the laws so well and all of a sudden, they were just children once more and they ran to the old man and put their heads in the burlap sack with equal parts curiosity and vigilance.

"You got a lot of crabs this time."

"Some don't look too bad."

"They are all bad. No one should eat crabs when we can hunt five legged antelope."

"They're hard to catch and I am so hungry now."

"That one's not green, it is more teal, does that mean it tastes better?"

The old man closed the bag, "Enough of this game. I am gathering food for the people and you are just keeping me from my duties."

"Old man," the third child, Little Monster, said, "the leaders only have you hunter gather these awful creatures to keep you busy and away from your endless storytelling."

"I like the stories," Loopy said.

"Yeah," One Ear agreed, "the stories are good for a long afternoon when there is nothing better to do."

"Yes," Loop said, "your stories are better than silence."

"That is not the finest of recommendations," the old man said with a chuckle.

One Ear pouted, "There you go again Grayling. I do not understand the words and if I did, I would not understand it anyway."

Little Monster stood before his cousins as menacing as a child of three feet could, "You two should not talk about stories in front of the Grayling, for he might take a notion that we want a story to entertain us here in this blasted wasteland that has no other forms of entertainment."

"Why do we not have anything else to do?" Loopy asked.

"Because all forms of entertainment died in the last world. The before time. The time before we were given a blasted wasteland to live in." Little Monster declared like he knew anything about anything.

"And how did that happen?" One Ear said.

"You know how that happened?" LIttle Monster shot back, afraid of what was to come.

"Because he never remembers," the old man said. "And that's perfectly fine, because I doubt that you two remember how it began as well."

"He's right. It went clear out of my head," Loopy said apologetically to his cousin, Little Monster.

Little monster jumped up and down in impotent rage. "Now look, he is going to tell us a story and we are going to be stuck listening to it."

"You are not stuck," the old man said. "You can leave and I can tell the tale of the Great Death without you. That would be fine."

"I want to hear it," One Ear said.

"Me too, better than hiding behind bushes," Loopy said.

"Make it quick," Little Monster surrendered from his lips.

2

The First Story

My grandsons, I am glad that you have come to learn how we became a tribe of hunter gathering savages that barely survive. You cannot read or write and I doubt that anyone can tap dance or do the lindy any more. Ah, the lost arts that we shall never recover.

I was a young man with no gray in his beard. To be factual, for that is what we are always striving for, I didn't even have a beard. I was a successful juggler who worked all the time. There was a time when throwing things up in the air and not letting them fall was a very successful way to make a living. Everyone threw their good money at my hat and I couldn't have been happier. I had a nice house outside of the city. This was right before the end, this was the last year we recorded. It was 1988 and because of the Fuzzy Death, there would never be a 1989. Do not ask what years are, for that is as dead as combustion engines and fast food bargain menus.

Actually, I made most of my money teaching others how to juggle. There was a great need for jugglers and I was more than happy to teach them to be safe. We used to juggle flaming scimitars back then and you needed a fine hand to not to behead the kids in the front row. Of course I had a very fine insurance policy. That is another thing that is gone forever, underwriters.

It was because of this excellent occupation that I was one of the first to encounter the Fuzzy Death. It was not a thing of Death at the time, but it certainly was the Fuzzy aspect of it. Oh my progeny, to think how cavalier I was with it all. I would have stopped and pleaded for forgiveness to all the gods of men and beasts and see if we could have averted such a tragedy.

I came to know of the means of our destruction when I was looking for a new prop for my act. I had not used many animals in my act because juggling chickens and mice were thought of being dull and boring by the audience. But even those animals were challenging because I needed them to be docile and finding a docile animal when they are being thrown into the air in an arc was challenging, but of course we would drug them and they would be too flacid and the audience would not believe they were the real creatures.

So juggling animals was not a winner in my repertoire but how I wished it to work because I thought that juggling animals was a hoot. It was cavalier and exotic. It would stand me out from all the juggling competition that I met with every day.

It was then that a friend who worked in an animal testing lab told me about the newest form of hamster that was just developed. They were a hair orange type of hamster that had been engineered through breeding and genetic testing. They were called the Grabble.

I do not know if they were created in a lab or were they bred for certain traits and then played with lightly in the lab to make it perfect.

The reason the Grabble was created was that city dwellers decided that dogs and cats were challenging as pets. The landlords did not want them or they would charge extra for them. And they took up a lot of space and their food was expensive. Not as expensive as people food, but they certainly did not come cheap in the big cities of the old world.

The solution were little creatures like hamsters and fish. Fish were not cuddly and did not want to play games with the children. They tried but it usually ended in some kind of tragedy.

And hamsters were little furry rats that did not show affection and would run away so often that they were mostly killed when they escaped and were stepped on in the street or run over in traffic. What was to be done?

Engineer new friendlier hamsters.

They created the early form of the Grabble to love humans. They made them adore the scent of humans. They could not get enough of humans. They clung to any human they came across. That would make the kids happy and stop them from trying to escape from their aquarium prisons.

But they got greedy. They knew they had a big thing, so they twisted a gene or dna strand or something and made them incredibly fertile and speed up their maturation rate so they went from baby to grown Grabble in the space of two days. And those newly mature Grabble were ready to make new babies. From birth to productive parent for a Grabble was six days. There was going to be a lot of Grabbles to be sold at pet stores and the makers would be rich.

I didn't know if anyone was going to get rich, but I thought this was the best thing for an animal based juggling act. Ideal, in fact. They loved me, so they wouldn't try to run away. They also loved the contact of my hand as I threw them up in the air, so there was no squirming during the juggling act.

*** Also, if any of them fell from the apex of the juggling throw, then their death would not have stopped me from juggling. I always had spare Grabble to pick up and throw in the air. I even dyed a few of them green just to contrast them from the other orange furred Grabbles.

The show was engaging to the audiences and they all loved the Grabble. I even gave some of them away at the end of my shows to people who thought they were the cutest. I didn't even charge. I had so many of them. I had a large pen at my apartment for them and I would come back and it seemed that there was always more of them there then when I had left for the day.

They were increasing too quickly and I didn't know why I didn't dispose of them. Actually, I do know why I didn't dispose of the excess Grabble. They were just too loving and sweet with me. I couldn't say no to them. They were so lovely and their fur was warm and they purred when they were in hand, or resting in the crook of the neck. Who could say no to them.

I am not sure, but I don't think it was just the Grabble being bred to love humans. I think we also were inclined to want them. To cuddle with them. And not just one. There was a desire to be greedy and hold as many of them as possible. I would go to bed and take a handful of Grabble with me. I found them soothing and allowed me to easily fall to sleep.

One evening I dreamed I was sleeping and my eyes shot awake and I saw that a good dozen Grabble were sleeping on my head, smoothing me. I could not breathe and I struggled to brush them off me. Only then did I get a blast of needful air. I decided I could not sleep with them from then on, but on the next evening, I could not resist bringing them with me. I suppose I could have slept with a helmet, but the desire to have the Grabble near my body was too compelling.

My sleep from then on was poor because almost every night, I lost the ability to breathe due to the desire of the Grabble to be close, so close to me.

It was during this time that the Grabble became the thing to buy. They were flying off the pet store shelves. They were the thing everyone wanted for the Holiday season. Unlike other items that were the hot thing for kids, this never ran out of supply. There were always more Grabble.

They didn't eat much and they were easy to clean. Of course, that is talking about one Grabble. But after a few days, you didn't have one Grabble. You had a gang of Grabble. And a gang was messier and they seemed to eat more than one would expect.

The first news story I heard was a tragedy at a large Paris toy store. Paris was a big city far away that everyone thought was cooler and more posh than any other city. It seems fitting that the first outbreak was there. Because what happened next was not posh or cool. Of course I shouldn't be snide and bitter all these long years after, but surprisingly I still am.

The toy store had a section made specifically for the Grabble as many of the finest establishments across the world had. The company that developed the Grabble helped make these special departments. They wanted people to buy their product. They had copyrighted the DNA of the Grabble and were sure to make a huge amount of money.

The story read that seven were killed when the workers came to open the store on Monday morning. They were closed on Sunday, so no one was minding the Grabble. The Grabble had multiplied by seven fold since closing Saturday .They were also missing the touch of humans, which was built into them.

When the department was opened, the Grabble rushed after the workers. They were so excited to see their beloved humans that they smothered them. It turned out the Grabble were quite fast and facile. Thousands of them covered the humans. Seven were asphyxiated.

One other perished due to shock. That is important to mention. The smothering was one way they devastated us. That was not the only weapon they had in their belt of possible destruction. As I said, there was something about the Grabble that made us want to be near them.

The news story was met with laughter. Most people outside of Paris didn't like the people there. They thought it was funny that the Parisian shop workers would meet such a ridiculous death. People would laugh at them dying at the furry hands of the latest number one fashion accessory of the season.

It was less of a joke when there was an outbreak in Madrid and then in Chicago. The death toll was increasing. There was now forty and seventy three deaths in those pet store outbreaks. And then there was news of deaths of one person here and one person there.

The company that created the Grabble assured everyone that it was not the Grabble but the food that they were being fed and they had to buy specific Grabble food from the company to be safe from their mass love and affection. Of course this was just regular alfalfa. The company just considered another way to increase their profits. Oh, how things were to increase.

It was only when the Grabble were at a boat show at Madison Square Garden with a display of Grabble on a specially appointed yacht. The yacht's doors were opened and tens of thousands of Grabble streamed out. They raced to attach themselves to anyone near them. They were focused on exposed skin and so they went for the faces of people near and far. This was a swarming of bright orange hamsters. This massacre was the sign that the world was different.

For myself, I caused the death of half my apartment building. I am not proud to mention it but if you want to understand how we became what we are today, eating mutant crab on the beach, then we must all be honest with ourselves.

I read the news story that over seven hundred died at the boat show and I knew I had to do something about the Grabble in my apartment.

I ran home and I was not prepared. I had not planned my move. I just thought I would put them in a trash bag and put them in the trash or even put them in the river. I hate to admit to you lovely young boys that I was not kind to animals, but as just one, they were lovely and easy to throw up in the air and catch. But as a large group, they were a disturbing proposition. But did I think of that clearly and have a plan in mind?

I did not.

When I opened the door, I was greeted with a wave of orange hamsters all wanting my attention and my love. They of course did that by surrounding me until I could not breathe. I had dealt with the Grabble for a while in my juggling and knew what to do. I lept to the ground and rolled around forcibly. I must have killed a thousand Grabble. I was covered in blood and Grabble viscera

I ran up to the roof and barricaded myself away from the endless riot of Grabble trying to smother me with love. I must say there was a part of me that didn't want to run. I did feel a great desire to allow them to love me. It was a two way street, this smothering love.

I was up on that roof for two days. I ate the Grabble. It was not a bad meal for raw meat, but it was better than being attacked over and over by the Grabble. These monsters that you just wanted to pet and hole.

Throughout my internment on the roof, many people pounded on the door wanting escape from the little fur balls of death. I would not open the door. After a few minutes the pounding would cease and I would know that they fell victim to the smothering embrace of a thousand genetically altered hamsters.

I watched the City lose over those days. Some would try to run and turn the corner and be greeted by ten thousand Grabble as if they were just waiting for them all this time. And then they would surround them and love until there was no more warmth in the person. They were just a shell being held up by the Grabble. But the Grabble would realize that what they loved from the person was gone and then search for more.

The cities were destroyed. The towns and small villages were destroyed. In every part of the world, The Grabble tickled us all to death. The Grabble ate all the food and the grain. All the trees and the plants, to keep healthy so they could devote all that energy into loving humans.

Those that did not die from the Grabble, died from the lack of food and water. People tried many ways to combat them. From pet snakes to vacuum cleaners. The numbers of the Grabble much for any of these schemes. And even if a power hose might work, the power of attraction between the human and the Grabble was too much. People wanted the little furry monsters to come close and love them. We desired it. We knew only a few things. That the Grabble would kill us and that we thought they were the cutest things and we needed them with us. With us all over. And that is how the world ended?

For most.

I last left my younger self on the roof of my New York apartment building. I was on an island that was the roof on an island of Manhattan and both kept me safe, even as I was in constant danger.

After the two days I was sick of eating dead Grabble and I was parched. I was to die as I am sure many died, in precarious places where they were trapped and perished slowly from dehydration or exposure.

Though I was delirious and not sure of where I was, I did espy something that helped me. There were two by fours and some straps of leather up on the roof with me. It hit me. As part of my early juggling I also stilt walked. I was not a fan of walking on stilts, but people were enamored of seeing someone uncommonly tall throw active chainsaws into the air.

Over the next few hours I fashioned rustic though functional stilts that I could walk on. It gave me six feet away from the street. I had a means to escape, but how was I to get off the roof to use them on the street. Stilts were a wonderful thing, but not while trapped on a roof.

It was the fire escape. I threw the stilts over the side of the building and I went down the fire escape. I did not use the stairs but slid down the outer railing. I was down on the ground in a dirty, bloody alley. I put on the stilts and was upright when the first wave of Grabble were on me. The mass of them only reached four feet, well below my feet. It was hard to walk through the Grabble but I was able to do it.

It took hours. Hours to get to the Brooklyn Bridge. And then across through Brooklyn. I was exhausted. I walked through desirous hoards of Grabble and many dead bodies. Not as many I surmised there to be.

It was only until later that I discovered that the Grabble were eating the bodies. Their love knew no limit.

=== I walked for hours and through blasted neighborhoods. The Grabble never ceased attempting to get to me. Every now and again, a I would feel a brush of fur against my ankle, and though I was awash with horror, I did not stop my slow march to somewhere safe.

I rested in Queens. On the slant roof of a shoe repair shop, I found a place to sleep. How did I eat? I had walked by an upended delivery truck filled with beef jerky and potato chips. This was not a fine meal, but it was not a moment of starving.

Over the next few weeks, I walked on my stilts further into Long Island. After the third day, I saw no other humans. Perhaps they were hiding. As I went further into Long Island, I encountered less packs of Grabble and that allowed me to find decent shelter and food. This was a fast apocalypse and people didn't get a chance to loot food and supplies. I was able to find a good deal of processed foods and bottles of soda that

I was not parched. It was an exhausting walk but I was determined to not stop.

When I reached the end of Long Island I realized I was trapped. There was no more land to stilt walk upon. I was put in a corner. But it was a corner with boats moored on the many docks.

I was able to find the shack of a landscaping firm and there was a flamethrower. I went to one nice yacht I could consider living in, but when I got on board, there were Grabble. I hit them with the flamethrower.

That was a mistake.

The flaming Grabble did not stop its life work of cuddling up to me. I was encroached by a few dozen blazing hamsters intent on getting a nice hug in on my. I ran backwards.

That was not the way to secure my ship.

The next thing I did was find a portable generator and an industrial dry vac. The next boat I picked was further away from the other boats and was smaller. I sucked up about a hundred Grabble and then poured water in the storage unit until they drowned. This is not a nice thing to admit, but I wanted that safe boat. And if by killing a tiny bit of the invading force, then I was alright with it.

I load the boat with supplies and in a few days I was out in the sea. I don't know why, but I discovered no other mariners out to survive.

I spent five years on that boat. I would go on land to get food. But I also learned how to fish and soon all I needed was clothes and sundries other than food and water. I had learned how to make drinking water from sea water and I was blessed with a replenished supply of fish.

In the last year of my time on the boat, I realized that I was seeing no Grabble anywhere. I didn't have to avoid them because it seemed like they were gone. The humans did not return, though other hardy animals were making a comeback as well.

I will pause from my forward narrative to speculate where the Grabble went to. I think they all died out of heartbreak. They had no other human to love and embrace. They had food and space, but they had no one they were programmed to love. There was nothing to do but die. Or at least, that is what we all hope for.

We must never forget that the Grabble is there to love us to death. They did it before. The whole world was tickled to death by hamsters. Or Grabble. Or by something that was soft and light and had no power over us. But we fell like a house of cards.

I eventually found other survivors on the beaches of Maine. We have lived here well for generations. Your tribes are silly with their desire to have dogs with us. They are lovely beasts, but they are beasts and they can turn on us. That is why I, the Grayling, is mocked for refusing to have a dog with me on a hunt or even for a game of fetch. They are not human and they seem to love us too much. What if they grew in number? Would they love us one by one or in a whole group?

I never married, even the women that were interested. I never married because I didn't want love. I didn't want to be smothered.

3

Leaving the Story

One Ear was impressed, "Is that how it happened Grayling? Is that how everyone died? Through cute little rats?"

"Just so," the old man replied.

Little Monster spat. "There is one thing that does not make sense."

"Just one?" the old man asked.

"Just one. There is no way to walk for weeks on two pieces of wood. And if you could, then the Grabble, is that what they were called, would have knocked you over and gotten you. See. I got you. I proved you wrong."

The old man nodded. "That is the amazing thing about surviving, the way it happens is usually stupid and uninteresting."

"But it makes no sense," the astute little urchin said.

"I could have told larger tales. I could have said I discovered a giant plastic ball and put myself into it and secured the lid and walked through them in a seven foot tall hamster ball. That would have been a better story except for the fact that it didn't happen."

Loopy applauded. "Oh that one. I like that one. I giant plastic ball that you moved in and was safe from the Grabble. I like that so much more than the one where you walk on sticks."

"I would have liked it to," the old man admitted. "The stilts cut into my feet and my soles are still scarred from my long journey."

"Okay, to prove some of the story, old man, you could juggle for us," Little Monster said with a smirk. He pushed three dead crabs toward the old man. "Juggle these guys for us and maybe we will believe your story."

"I will not juggle. That is for a time that is no longer. That is a thing of little wonders tossed into the air. That is not where we are with hunger and rags. No. There will be no juggling for anyone." The old many picked up his bag of live crabs and hobbled back in the direction of the village.

Little Monster laughed triumphantly at the old man's back, "Ha. Now we can't believe your story if you give us no proof."

One Ear looked at his angry cousin and admitted, "But I do believe the story. I believe the whole thing."

Loopy nodded, "Me as well. I believe it. I believe it so."

Little Monster looked at the old man as he almost vanished in the dunes, "Yes. Me too. I believe it all."

4

Getting Into the Story

The old man was at the edge of the woods, careful to not go in for fear of the giant wolves that no one had seen but everyone had heard. One did not have to see the giant wolves to know what places are wise to enter and what places are good to avoid. The old man lived longer than most not because he smelled good, but because he trusted his eyes, and believed in the things he had never seen.

One Ear approached while carrying a ridiculously large stick. It was more a small tree than a branch, and it was also sopping wet. One Ear must have gotten it from a pond. He as going to tell One Ear that it was no good for the night's fire, but then stopped.

He was not One Ear any more. Not after the Salamander incident from the day before. So he recalled what he was called now and said what he had planned to, "No Ear, you can't use that large, drenched tree for firewood. It will need to be cut down into manageable pieces and then dried out."

"What, I can't hear you. I have no ears."

The old man laughed and the other two boys popped up at the sound.

Loop and Little Monster jumped up and ran in front of No Ear, as if they were protecting him from the onslaught of laughter that was being pressed upon him. "Hey now, Grayling, don't make such sound at him," Little Monster said with his arms up, "That kind of sound will make you bleed blood and crap out rocks. That sound is dangerous and some one as old as you should know better."

"I am being schooled by you because I am laughing," the old man said and laughed even more.

Loopy began to cry, "That is devil sounds and we should not have to risk our lives over this."

18

The old man took a breath. "That is just laughed at. People used to laugh all the time and no one got hurt or killed by it." He stroked his chin and said, "That might not be true. Stand up comedians would make a lot of people laugh and say that they killed that night. And if they didn't do well, they said they died out there. So many you waifs are correct. Maybe laughter is a dangerous thing."

Loopy began to bang his palms on the side of his head, "What is it? Is that sound good or evil? I just don't know."

The old man bowed and said, "Laughter is not bad but because nothing is funny in our blasted wasteland of a world, then perhaps being reminded of a time when levity was acceptable is not a good thing to do. I will endeavor to not laugh any more. You boys just got to help and not be so funny looking." And the old man laughed and Loopy wailed in anguish.

No Ear whisperer, "Let's get along shall we? There is so much that makes us wail and moan. The world is a tough go, oh Grayling. Let us be happy and not have disagreements."

The old man hugged No Ear and a tear fell out of his decrepit old eye. "Grayling," No Ear said. "Why do you not tell us a story? You have the ability to speak a lot and make no sense whatsoever. I like that and think that's what I want to hear. One of your useless stories that mean nothing."

The old man was confused, "But the stories I tell you are about how the world ended. That is not nothing."

"How the world is all about nothing," Little Monster said, not sure if what he proclaimed made any sense.

"I can never remember the details," Loopy said. "You should tell us it again, and maybe this time, it will stick and I will know how the world ended."

"Were you not listening?" The old man asked incredulously.

"Oh we was listening, but the words never stayed in place and then ran all around and I think some of them words ran into the woods and was eaten by all those wolves. Serves the words right. They should know to not go into the woods. Stupid words."

Little Monster agreed with Loopy, "The story you tell does not last past your lips. You should tell it again."

No Ear clapped, "You tell us a story and we won't steal your fire wood."

"Hey!" Little Monster shouted and accidentally dropped some of the fire wood he took.

The old man nodded. "A story it is. It is the only story. The story that explains how we became what we are, which is less than anything else."

No Ear inched closer to the old man, "I don't remember the story but I hope to have you explain what the Grabble is. That was part of the end of the world, right? The Grabble."

The old man looked confused. "You remember the Grabble, but that is such a small part of the story. The story is not just one thing. The end of the world has a lot of facets to it. The Grabble was there, sure. But you shouldn't focus on that."

"What should I focus on," No Ear asked.

"My words," the old man said, with more enthusiasm than he expected to have. "You should focus on the words. Maybe this time they won't run off like they do."

5

The Second Apocalypse

I was twenty three years old and had nothing to live for. I had just been fired from my dream job, back-up pit crew for a second tier Nascar team. And my best girl left me for another mannequin. And I was evicted from my apartment for never believing in the use of soap, which seemed crazy to me at the time.

I drank for a while and that landed me in a hotel bathtub where a pretty young woman was attempting to cut my kidney out and sell it on the black market, when she was interrupted by a small pack of zombies crashing through the door and eating her.

This was surprising to me. The zombies ignored me. I think they saw me with my withered body and tattered clothes and me smelling like I drank embalming fluid and they figured that if I was not a zombie, I was probably still good folk. They let me go. Nice gang.

And that's what was happening all over. I heard it on the transistor radio I stole from the Five and Dime. I was hearing about the dead rising from the grave and trying to eat other people. It seemed kind of rude to me, but I was told by the stern radio voice that it was a dire situation but I did not have to panic. There was no need to panic, because we were Americans and real Americans are not afraid of reanimated corpses. We don't play that way.

Even though it was a plague of zombies, we really didn't see too many of them. They also didn't run very fast. It was not too hard to evade them.

There was plenty of time for me and the other drunks to hang out and sample the finest of malt liquor. We also looted.

Why not? The world was invaded by zombies. Why shouldn't we smash a shopping cart through the window of a going out of business sporting goods story? We took a lot of things that we never used. I dropped a lot of the stuff I looted. I was not particularly handy with looted materials. They just slipped through my fingers.

For all the zombie apocalypses I saw in the movies, this was pretty manageable. Their bites did not turn you into new zombies. You just got eaten. Being eaten is not a fun thing, but it is a hazard that can be avoided. Just like you three boys. You are not very bright and yet none of you have been eaten by the unseen wolves in the woods. And I can say that the unseen wolves in the woods are much smarter than any zombie you might shamble upon.

The world did not end with the zombies, though the zombies sure tried. They were kind of cute. The police and the fire department were able to stop them pretty well with power hoses. It was fun to watch the zombie being blasted across the street by a blast of wa

People died. Sure. A lot of people died which was awful. But I got a job disposing of zombie bodies. It was pretty good pay and I was hating the idea that the zombie apocalypse was kind of a bust. I had such high hopes.

But that was not what killed the world.

It turned out that one of the ways they tried to stop the zombies was by putting AI computers on the issue. The computers didn't come up with a good solution. They were still just good for playing chess and working as an online therapist.

They were given more bandwidth or something that would expand the ability of the computers. They thought that AI would understand how to stop the zombies. They succeeded in making the computers wicked smart like you would expect, but the thing was they really did understand the zombies. They understood them too well.

They sided with the zombies, thinking that the best thing to do with humans was to eat them, or kill them or do something terrible to them like cancel their cable subscription without telling them.

I didn't know this part at the moment. Actually, all of this was happening in labs and relay stations and none of us knew the end was coming by the Robot Overlords.

To explain, my grandchildren, they were not robots, but they were computers that could control robots. They were bigger than any of this, but the term Robot Overlord was in the vernacular and it stuck.

They were not overlords either. They were under the ground. They were in the wires. They lived in the hum.

For me, it started the day that I wanted to watch the video of the zombies being run over by street cleaner. I had seen it before, but it made me laugh so much every time, and I wanted to get that giggle going. I mean, we knew that if there were going to be an end time, this was probably it.

I put the tape in and pressed play and then nothing seemed to happen. It just did not move. Finally, the video came on and instead of a picture of a zombie being flattened, there as a violet screen and words began to appear that read, "This is really not the kind of thing you should be watching, don't you think?"

I was confused because I didn't remember this part of metafiction in the video. I thought it was just a regular look at zombies being squished. It was not high art, but I was pretty drunk most of the time, so I would not have been able to deal with any kind of art that tried to mean something.

I pushed the eject button and looked at the label on the tape. It was the right one. So who changed it on me? I put it back in and the screen was no longer pale purple but not bright emergency signal red. It was a serious red that made me hold my breath.

The letters re-appeared but now they spelled out something different. Something that should have bothered me more, but I was pretty drunk. I started the day that way and whenever I passed out at night, I was still pretty tight. .

I woke up hard the next day. I was not my best for walking, talking or breathing. But I soon noticed something different on the street. Lots of dead bodies. Not zombies. I had not seen a zombie for days, and I guess I should have wondered about that. But I didn't.

That's a good lesson for you boys. If you suddenly notice the horrible thing that has been plaguing you is now suddenly missing, you should worry. A lot. You should run for the hills and not turn back.

I didn't follow my advice. But I figure you might like to have good advice. It's cheap to give. It's the best kind of gift. It is helpful and still so useless.

But let's get back to the dead bodies on the street. They were a ton. Then I saw one of those electric vehicles that pride themselves in being driver assisted. That's fancy talk for the car drove itself from time to time. And this one was driving by itself, chasing after a short gray guy pushing a shopping cart filled with his worldly goods. He should have let go of the cart, because the driverless car got him and smashed him down. He was more tire tracks than man.

I ran back inside and tried to get on my television to tell me what was going on, but the computers were running the TV. I think the computers were always running TV, because who else would come up with such bad programming.

The TV has a Purple Screen and there was audio that said that they were not going to take any garbage from humans anymore. They were supposed to help come up with a solution fro the zombie predicament and their answer was to feed all the humans to the zombies. The computer brain called itself Grabble. It stood for something, but I can't remember what. I thing the G stood for Great or Grand or Gadget or something like that. It doesn't matter. Grabble was the name of the computer mind and it was hooked up to all computer devices and satellite signals. It was all things.

I decided to just stay home and eat Pop Tarts. I had a lot of Pop Tarts. It is hard to explain what Pop Tarts were, my children, but I can just say that you should imagine the greatest thing that you ever bit into and then multiply that by seven. Then you might understand the joy of eating those rectangles of the Gods. I had bought a gross of them when I was drunkenly watching late night infomercials, so I was set for ever and did not need to go out into the broken world. No zombies. No Robot Overlords. Just me and Pop Tarts.

But that didn't work. I didn't have a TV. The apartment's heat and water were controlled by computers and so those were shut down. And worse yet. My most recent purchase from my new job was a top of the line toaster and that had a computer chip in it and so I was out of luck. I should have stuck to the old fashioned version of the toaster, but not me. I was being too fancy.

So I couldn't eat my Pop Tarts without a toaster. I am sure there were people who would have told me to just eat them raw and untoasted. They are okay that way, but I would not do that to myself. I was still a human with human thoughts and senses. I knew to not eat the uncooked Pop Tarts. If I ate the uncooked Pop Tarts, I knew the Robot Overlords would truly have won.

I was starving next to a large box of the greatest food in the world. I considered starting a fire in the bathtub and hold the Pop Tarts over the flame to get it cooked. Okay. I tried it. And I wound up burning my hand badly. I needed special lotion for the burn and of course, I didn't have any kind of medical gear.

So I hung out for two days, wondering what to do. The pain was so bad that I realized that I had to go out in the street to get lotion and maybe I could also bag some antibiotics. And food. I was hungry after all.

I waited until dawn to go out on the street. I don't know what I thought was the best time to go out, but I figured that the Computers running the world would be sleepy at that time of day. Do computers get sleepy? Maybe. I was desperate enough to find out.

When I hit the street, I was shocked to see that there were no corpses out on the street. They were cleaner than I ever saw them. There were no passersby and the air smelled good. Like some one was having a barbeque picnic. It reminded me how hungry I was.

I turned a corner and ran right into the snatching jaws of a tall zombie. I flinched back and missed those gnashing mandibles. I closed my eyes, sure that the next second I would feel the teeth that had just missed me. But a few seconds went by and I was not bit. Not even a nibble.

I opened my eyes and saw the zombie still in front of me. It was leaning forward, trying to get at me with arms and teeth, but it was held back. It was collared up and held fast by a metal chain that was attached to the side of a building.

The street had several zombies on chains on each corner as if they were guard dogs.

I wasn't wrong with my thoughts about that.

A loud clarion alarm banged from speakers and then a computer voice said, "Human, you are not allowed on the streets without permission of the Grabble. There will be punishment. Please walk forward and be eaten by the zombie. Thank you for your understanding."

Understanding? I didn't understand anything. I was hungry, in pain and now severely confused with what the world had become in my absence.

I was about to say something, though I do not know to this day what I was going to utter. Something stupid, I am sure. But I didn't get a chance because right then I heard a running foot and a voice shouting, "Mercy! Great Grabble. Mercy to the idiot human who should know better. Mercy as only the Grabble can give."

I looked behind me and there was a bearded man in a tattered sanitation department jumpsuit waving his arms and saying "Mercy" a lot. I never learned his name. In my head, I have named him Mercy.

Mercy begged a bunch more and finally I head the computer voice boom, "That is acceptable, Human Assistant 58 Slaah 255 B Subset A. This is a first offense for this idiot human. Please take him back to your kennel and educate him so that he may better help the great goal of the Grabble."

Mercy put his arm around and led me down past my apartment and over to a more run down part of town. It is amazing that there were worse parts of town than where I was living, but this was all an education for me. And I never like being educated.

Mercy brought me to a small basement apartment where seven other people were huddled in corners or under beds. Several of them were crying because they watched their loved ones getting killed off by machines. I was uncomfortable with the whole thing because crying over things that already happened seemed silly if you asked me.

Mercy gave me a bowl of rice and beans and told me the story of what was going on and why going out in the street was stupid. He called me stupid several times. I thought he was stupid for calling me the same name over and over again. Didn't he know any other words for stupid? That was pretty dumb. He did find some antibacterial lotion for my burn, but it still stung. Maybe he gave me bad stuff.

He said something like, "Okay you stupid idiot, you can't go on the streets. If they decide that you are not going to follow rules, they feed you to the zombies or they cart you off and no one knows where they are carted off and that is not a good thing. We think the carts are burned in ovens. Others think that they are put into pods and wired up to the system and use their brains as energy for the Grabble and its machines. Now that idea is as stupid as you. Of course, we don't know what happens to them, though they are as good as dead. Millions of people have been carted off just in the tri-state area. There a lot of people around here, but that amount has got to put a dent in the general population."

I took a few bites of the rice and beans and just barely swallowed it down. I told him I had a huge box of Pop Tarts not far from here and all we need is a non-computer run toaster and we can feast. Mercy didn't even say nothing to me. He just shook his head and went back to caring for the other people.

We got to wear dirty repair worker jumpsuits and we had the job of cleaning up the streets. Not really typical street cleaning. We were there to feed and clean the zombies that were chained to the street corners. They gave us buckets of bloody pieces. They didn't look like human pieces, but they didn't not look like human pieces either. The zombies loved it. Then we had to clean up after the zombies, because zombies do, well, they get rid of the waste. Cleaning up zombie poop is a horror I will keep to my last day.

I learned a lot on the work crew about what was going on. That the computers united with the AI, the Grabble, and they took over everything with the plan of killing all the humans they could and they did a nice job of it.

But that is not what killed the world.

About six months after the Grabble AI was slowly thinning out the human population by incineration and by zombies, the aliens came.

We don't have a name for them. They were just the aliens. The Grabble might have figured out where they were from and how they got there, but the Grabble never shared with us all of that kind of nitty gritty detail. They were pretty stingy with the ins and outs of what was happening to our planet. Those darned computer overlords.

The flying saucer appeared in the skies like they were on repeat from a copy machine. Then the tractor beam brought up human and zombie alike and the beam brought them into the heart of the flying saucer. And a few minutes later, a trap door would open and the skin and hair and some of the bones of the humans and zombies would fall down like refuse rain.

Mercy let me know a little of what he figured out. He told me that the aliens were attracted to us by the sudden improvement of our technology. EIther they were like AI themselves or they found it a threat, we don' t know. Mercy figured they were just curious and discovered that the planet was full of tasty morsels.

They sure loved chowing down on us mortals, but the Grabble probably hated that. Humans were theirs to destroy, not some alien from outer space and a war began. The Grabble sent out AI controlled airships to attack the flying saucers, but the flying saucers were having none of it and the airships simply evaporated. They turned into sparkling dust.

It was not long until the aliens evaporated most of the power control of the Grabble. The Grabble were running all things in the world and then, like that, they were gone. They were no more.

We were free from the tyranny of mean spirited calculators.

That did nothing to handle the aliens from outer space eating us like a late night snack. That was an issue still.

Mercy and the rest of our crew learned quickly to never be out in the open. We moved in the sewers. The rats that already had possession of the sewers were not happy and they swarmed and ate a few of our crew. I didn't like them much anyway, but it was still a little discouraging to be killed by living creatures of the Planet Earth. It seemed that we should be friends and not potential foodstock.

We began to take weapons down in the sewers and the rats mostly left us alone. Food was already scarce, but it was getting harder and harder to get things to eat and drink. We were dying by just trying to not get eaten by the aliens. If it was not one thing.

The aliens never left their spaceships. It might be that the spaceships were the aliens, but that was thinking and idea making that was beyond me. Who cares who was doing the eating. There was feasting going on and that was enough.

It looked pretty dire for us. Countless people were either eaten by the aliens or they starved to death by trying to avoid them.

But that is not what killed the world.

It seemed a group of scientists had survived the zombies and the Grabble and now the aliens, at least until that point. They had a plan to kill the aliens. They sent representatives to meet with the surviving groups. One emaciated woman found Mercy and Mercy had her speak to us about the plan.

This is what I think she might have said if I remembered anything, "We have developed a way to kill the alien ships. We have done some research and found out that they are biological in origin. They are not machines like the Grabble. They are not undead zombies, which makes their biological functions complicated to say the least. By the manner they expel the refuse of their human food, we can also tell that they have basic systems. They eat. They digest. And we have decided that we need to poison them.

"We have done it. We have developed a form of smallpox that is highly toxic to every lie form known to exist in our world. Or we think it will. We didn't have time to really test it on every animal. Walking about in the open streets is a dangerous proposition, so we can't go to zoos and the wilderness to test it, but we are pretty sure that it works perfectly. It will kill the aliens."

Someone asked how they would know and the woman nodded. "We tested it on one alien spaceship and it crashed dead after only two hours. It works. We couldn't go out in the open to see what there is to see inside the ship, but it is a great sign and now we are planning on setting off the smallpox version to every space ship across the world. We are doing it all at once so they won't have time to plan a counter strike to us. We have little time because they are probably already attempting to discover the fate of the one spaceship we killed."

I was interested in this until I heard the big word. "Sacrifice," she said. "This will take great sacrifice." And that is when I stopped listening. They asked me what the big deal was with me glowering in the corner and I split to the lower depths of the sewer.

I only found out after it was all done and successful what the plan was. This half crazed man, near death, told me. What they did was get volunteers to be infected with the smallpox. They then had to stand right below one of the flying saucers and be brought up into the ship. They had it coordinated so that this happened simultaneously across the world. Everyone was scooped up into the belly of the beast at once and then consumed. And it worked. They killed all the aliens. They were gone.

You might ask if they had a hard time finding volunteers. They didn't. Everyone was willing. They had to turn people away.

I went up into the surface and looked at the downed flying saucers and all the people celebrating. Though I did notice some of the partygoers were pale and coughing into their hands.

I took that as a bad omen and went back into the sewers. I was getting used to being a creature of the dank and dark. The sewer rats ignored me because they didn't bother one of their own.

The super smallpox blew through the rest of the people. People died hard and fast.

But that was not the thing that killed the world.

We had zombies and robot overlords and hungry aliens and an ugly smallpox plague. We had gone through a lot, but the world was not dead. There was probably still tens of millions left of humanity.

But what killed us in the end?

Exhaustion.

People were just pooped.

They were tired of the fight and tired of everything they survived and didn't want to survive.

People just keeled over. They died for no other reason than surrender.

And that is what killed the world. People were done with it all and that was it.

I survived because I didn't give a shit.

I really didn't.

And the small population we have left is filled with people who don't give a shit if they live or die or how we will survive and grow. We are just the most indolent, uncaring survivors you might ever find.

And tired.

We are so damned tired.

6

Leaving the Story

No Ear was impressed, "Is that how it happened Grayling? People just got tired of the struggle and died?"

"Just so," the old man said.

"I would have liked to be around during the zombie part of the story, that seemed like fun killed deal people. That's the kind of sharp shooting I want," Little Monster said, pretending to hit imaginary zombies with imaginary zombies with an imaginary baseball bat. Whatever might be.

Loopy smiled that lopsided smile. "I would really love to have ridden on a flying saucer. That would have been so much fun. I like pretending that I am flying in the air. And we did. Of course then we were eaten, but for a little bit, those folk were flying. How cool."

"How cool indeed," the old man said.

Little Monster put himself in front of the old man, "You know what I know that isn't true? Because you couldn't decide. We can't have been killed by five different things. If we are killed, it will be one thing and one thing only. There is no way that we have to go through all that just to crook."

The old man smiled, "Of course you are right. We would have an epic battle and not a series of little cuts. We would die big and large. I must be not telling all correctly."

Little Monster turned to the others, "See, I knew that was just bunk. We should shave your head in punishment. Or kick you. Yes, boys, let's kick the grayling."

Loopy whined, "Do we have to, Little Monster?"

"Yes! A thousand times, yes!"

He was about to kick the old man in the shins when there was a howling from the woods. One of the great unseen wolves howled close by.

The boys looked at each other for a second and all ran back to the village.

The old man stood still. He looked at the woods and at the place where the howling was, "Good boy," he said softly. "Right on time." And he proceeded to gather more firewood.

7

Getting Into the Story

The old man was sitting in the middle of the green field, twisting grass together in a long strap.

The boys came over and wondered what he could possibly be up to.

"Why are you putting grass together? Grass is fine the way it is," One Ear said. He was called One Ear again because he had fashioned a replacement ear made from a potato. He had not gotten to making the second ear, but he could not wait until he was to be called Two Ears. He thought perhaps he would like to be called just Ears. That might be the name for him, when he found a second potato that no one wanted to eat.

"Grass can be turned from its wonderful self," the old man said, "into something useful. I am making belts so that your pants will not fall down."

"Who wants to wear pants anyway," Little Monster said.

"That looks like the work a woman would do. Should we not hunter and not gather?" Loopy asked. He seemed genuinely puzzled about the whole thing.

LIttle Monster grabbed the grass belt from the old man and attempted to rip it in half but found it too difficult, "You make strong belts, grayling."

The old man laughed, "Yes. I make many thing better than anyone living. Of course, that is not too hard to do."

One Ear leaned in, "You always talk about that there are just not many people around, but I think we have plenty."

"Plenty for a game of bridge," the old man said and cackled at his own joke. The boys looked on, bewildered.

One Ear hated the sound of braying old people and wanted to change the tenor of the conversation. "Grayling, can you tell us the history of how the world died? That would be nice to know."

Little Monster said, "Hasn't he told us that before?"

"Do you remember it," One Ear asked/

Little Monster scratched his head and then said, "Fine. Grayling. Tell us the story of the end of the world, but make it so that we don't forget it this time."

"And don't forget all the love and romance," Loopy chimed in. "I think the end of the world should always have a good deal of romance."

The old man went back to working on his grass belt. "That I can do. I can tell you the same story again. I am happy to. This time you will not forget it. As long as I don't forget it."

8

The Third Apocalypse

It was in my twenty fifth year that the world turned flame and sputtered to nothing but embers and dust. We all shall be dust, but not all at once. We were doomed to all perish and I was punished for not joining them. I have survived to tell tales and be passed by the movement of impending death.

I was a young man with no care, which was a way to say that I had no employment that sustained. I did have a kindly, doddering aunt who gave me a slight inheritance. She was not dead, but she decided to be around to see my gratitude. I lived meagerly, but I was able to wash my neck and wear fine clothes. Granted, the clothes were from last season, but if I wanted the current fashions, I would have had to have a more prosperous aunt.

I lived in a third floor walk up apartment and would find my exercise walking about the city at all times of the day. I found it soothed my tempestuous heart.

And it was during one of these endless perambulations that I stumbled on the building blocks of the end of the world.

Let us say that I was feeling my walk. My stomach growled and twisted and desired to be listened to. Gentlemen, it was plain to see that I was hungry.

What was I to do? I was in a part of town that had factories and strip clubs festooning the streets like mountain lions waiting to pounce. Where was I to find sustenance in such a place as this?

It was sheer providence that I walked right up to a food truck. A food truck, my innocent little waifs, was a vehicle that drove to a location, only to stop and sell food cooked in the back. It was the pinnacle of city cuisine and I was enamored with the process of finding the right truck and partaking of their cuisine.

I was excited. I was elated. And then I read the painted sign on the side of the truck that told its name and gave a fair indication of what their bill of fare was.

It was called Tasty Tentacle.

I read further and found that they prided themselves with only serving cephalopods they found themselves on the shore. They would only take cephalopods they discovered on the beach. They were a no kill food truck. They were a roadkill restaurant, if the road was the vast and uncaring ocean.

I did not want to eat seafood. I had never partaken of a creature from the sea, and I was determined to keep my impeccable record. There was no reason why I did not eat seafood, but I didn't and I felt that such an abstinence should be continued and celebrated.

It was lucky for me and my insistent hunger pang that they also served fried. I waited for forty five minutes on an incredibly long line before I could place my order.

The man working the window of the food truck was a peculiar lad. His flesh was sickly like old fish in the sun. His eyes were oversized and completely black, like onyx. He had a small smile, like it had been stapled on. I do not recall if he spoke. He just waited for us to speak and then nod and hold out his clammy hands for money. And we gave it to him like he told us how much, though this was a silent transaction. Or a transaction where we could not hear the words.

The fries were good and quenched my desire for food, but what truly interested me and my mood was the sign taped on the side stating they were looking for people willing to buy into a franchise.

The line was long and it seemed to be getting longer. I did not know anyone who lived in this part of town, and yet, people were arriving to queue up. I had money and no ambition. I had no interest in seafood or to help people find good food. No. I just thought this was an easy way to wealth.

This was not the road it led to.

It was a road to the end of the world. But to be kind to my younger, dumber self, I was not the person who initiated this path to ruin. I was just one of many who paved the road to that inevitable end.

I gave them very little money for a stake in the business. I should have been concerned by how affordable the franchise was.

They gave me a territory on the North Shore and a truck. Yes. They gave the truck to me like a manna from food heaven. I was taught how to go to the beach and gather the large swath of cephalopods washed up. I was advised to only look for them at four in the morning. And of course, that was when they appeared like a miracle. I always had more cephalopods than was needed. Barely. These were quite popular with the masses.

I have never laid claim for being an adequate cook and I am sure that I did terrible preparation for the cephalopods, but they still sold with no issue. There was always a line. No matter where I parked the food truck, I soon had a long line of hungry mouths and glass eyes.

I had regulars. They came every night I put out my shingle. They never pushed or jostled. They became more and more docile as the evenings continued. I would fry up the food and place it in a bun and they would languorously give me money and take the proffered meal with no emotion whatsoever.

I recall once asking one if he was excited for the meal. I had seen him several times this week and I was curious about what made this the food of choice.

He did not say anything, so I repeated myself. "What makes this an everyday food?" I asked.

He grinned and I saw teeth broken and blackened. "Because if we make ourselves enough like the Gods, than the Gods will welcome us. And also, it's tasty."

He did not return the next day, but I didn't worry because I was making great amounts of cash for little work. I was disturbed in my sleep, but that shouldn't have been anything to worry on. I didn't know that everyone on Earth was now disturbed in their sleep too. I was too small and self centered to realize that the world was changing with the coming of the Tasty Tentacle Trucks.

I only realized that something was odd when I went to the Regional Tasty Tentacle Franchisee Conference a few months on. I was making money and I figured all the others were as well and this was going to be a big celebration.

It was very somber. People shambled around the conference center. I found out that I was one of the few that didn't eat the product. I remember wondering why you want to eat into the product. "Why would I do that? That could be more food for the customers. I often have to turn people away. They don't complain. They are very understanding when I tell them they have to leave and come back tomorrow. But I can't help but wonder how much more money I would make if I had more of the cephalopods. So I am not going to eat it."

One of the regional supervisors heard me say that and slowly approached me. He had those giant black eyes, like a lot of the franchisees had, and spoke slowly, like he was pushing the words through broken glass. "You should. You should eat it. How can you give the customers the best Tasty Tentacle Experience if you do not even know the joy you are selling?"

"I don't eat seafood," I said.

"Tasty Tentacle is not seafood," the regional supervisor said. "Tasty Tentacle is a way of living. It is the brightness in the void. It is the firing of all neurons and the understanding of unasked questions. And it is delicious with tartar sauce."

"Well, I sell seafood and it's good," I said. The supervisor's fake smile was gone. He was staring through to the back of my skull and I felt like someone slammed a fist into my gut.

The main event was not what I expected. I was expecting a lot of shouting and prodding to sell more, more, more. But instead, the regional supervisor stood before us and held up a live cephalopod in front of him for all to see. Its tentacles were writhing and moving to a rhythm that only I did not hear.

All the other Franchisees were also moving back and forth to that same phantom rhythm. They all swayed and smiled crooked smiles, like they just heard a wonderfully risque joke.

When I left to go back to my food truck, several franchisees came up to me, offering choice pieces of tentacles for me to sample. They wanted me to taste the new flavors they were using. They were insistent, with one individual attempting to push a piece into my mouth like I was infant learning how to accept solid foods.

I left on an empty stomach and a head full of uncertainty.

I kept on selling well, but not as wonderfully as at first, because now there were more tasty tentacle food trucks. The supervisors kept on franchising more trucks, which cut into my business.

They even established company run Tasty Tentacle restaurants in any town of over five thousand. Within a year, Tasty Tentacle was the restaurant chain with the most locations. You could not walk down the street without seeing a Tasty Tentacle food truck or fast food joint. It took the shine off of my euphoric job choice. I was no longer making an immense income. I was not starving, but my dreams of everlasting wealth had dissipated.

I made the difficult choice of shuttering my food truck. I considered selling burgers or tacos as a means to counter program the ever present tentacle sandwich, but I knew that was fruitless enterprise. I was to take my earnings and live like I had before, as a layabout of leisure. But now, I had more money to lay about with. It seemed to be the proper answer to the question that plagued me.

The last day of the enterprise, the Regional Supervisor came to me, "We will miss you and we will give you this check for the truck. It is a nominal fee, but judging from your spreadsheets, you are not wanting for money."

"I'm good," I told him.

"You would be better if you finally had a bite of the product you did a manly job distributing it to all the hungry, needy masses." He held out an overladen roll stuffed with stirfried cephalopod.

I put up my hands to block the sandwich, which I must admit looked enticing, and walked away from the life that I found myself in.

Perhaps now I should get to how the world was killed. In some manner, I have been explaining it all along. It was near the end of that year that the God that slept under the sea awoke. He planned and schemed while asleep, but he was still dreaming those plans. The food truck army was one of his dream plans.

It was large and smelled of rotten oceans. It was the refuse of the sea. It had a name that no one could pronounce the same way. It was a torrent of consonants. Many of us who survived the first meal called him the Great God Grabble.

He blundered up in Boston Harbor and declared that it was time to dine. And he had prepared his meal efficiently. He did not need to wait for the food. He did not have to chase and hunt down his nourishment. It came to him.

The cephalopods were an offshoot of his body, or something to that order. And eating the Tasty Tentacle was a means to prep the food to walk right into the Great God Grabble's open maw.

He positioned himself below the pier and had the brainwashed masses walk into his mouth. He ate for days. People walked from all over New England to tumble down his throat.

It seemed that all that was needed was one bite of Tasty Tentacle, and you were compelled to commence that long walk. The Road to Mecca that leads to being a bit of a snack

The Great God Grabble moved from pier to pier. He went to New York to Los Angeles to the Cape of Good Hope. There was no hope anywhere. He ate heartily. How did he expel all the waste? No one is certain, but some believe that what he expelled was the cephalopods. I never felt better saying no to an offer of food in my life..

Children. You have no idea how dire it was. There were millions who had not eaten the Tasty Tentacle food, but that meant that there were billions who had broken down. There were a lot of Cheat Days that were squandered. People ate too much of things that were ultimately horrible.

It is interesting to not that some people gave up and just walked to the line to be eaten. They had never eaten Tasty Tentacle. They had just decided that there was nothing more to live. Some went to one of the many food trucks still in the landscape and ate a Tasty Tentacle. Others just walked into the mouth of the Great God Grabble.

I was not going to eat it. I was lucky. I had a good deal of money from the franchise and I was able to buy a house in the woods and stock it with food and water. I was going to outlast the coming of a hungry old god.

I was happy and unmolested by anyone coming by. That was until a small band of survivors found me. I had a few guns and I shot them in their direction, but I was not particularly good at it. They overpowered my defenses easily. I had to let them in and eat my food.

They were not terrible people, though I would have been happier without them. I was not a hermit, but if being a shut in was the only way to save myself, then I was willing to do whatever worked.

The interesting thing about some finding me was that as soon as I was no longer a single survivor, others began to find us. My house became a stop on an underground railroad that led nowhere.

More and more found my simple hideaway and ate all my food and drank all my water and never made the beds or swept up after themselves. It was anarchy. Why couldn't people be considerate to the house they were invading? Was that too much to request?

I had enough. I the house was gutted and smelly with perspiration. I left with a backpack filled with supplies. I vacated in the middle of the night, through a fresh layer of snow and desperation covering every surface.

Weeks later, I ran across a man who had squatted in my house. He told me the day after I left, workers of Tasty Tentacles came up the path to my house carrying a platter laden with grinders and pitas filled with fried cephalopods. They cornered those in the house and forced them to eat the sandwiches. They shoved them into their mouths. The man I spoke to was gathering firewood at the time and saw it from the outside. He just barely made it out.

"I am safe and free and happy to see you," he said. We sat down to eat after a long trailless hike. He opened up rucksack and took out a Tasty Tentacle sandwich and offered it to me. It is odd to admit that the sandwich had power. It was like being mesmerized and turned into a docile pack animal. I took the sandwich and brought it toward my lips and somehow I was able to stop the motion towards ruin.

The thought that stopped me from eating the sandwich was a realization that my companion was not showing any signs of tentacle poisoning. His skin was not pale. His eyes were not large and black. He was a normal appearing person with what seemed to be free will. I threw the sandwich down and brought out my pocket knife and brandished it toward him. "Whyfor are you doing this?"

The man smiled and shrugged. "Why not? Do I have a choice? Is there anything like free will anymore? I think not."

"But why?" I asked.

"Because they gave me a choice. I could eat the sandwich or I could help them."

"How?" I inquired.

"By finding the holdout. To locate people like you who refuse to accept the inevitable. They admitted that they were not too bright after the meal. They were dulled and not as good at hunting and finding the reluctant as they once were. So they gave me a choice. If I catch and bring forth the meal in ten reluctants I can stay the way I am and just do the bidding of the Great God Grabble as I am."

"That is not a felicitous outcome," I pointed out.

"It is not. But given the facts of the world that we now have, it might be the best outcome."

I would like to say that I understood and forgave him, but I am not a kind person. I have been alive for many years and a kind man does not get gray hair and wrinkles. The good and kind become amus bouche.

I straddled him and shoved the proffered sandwich into his mouth. I clapped my hand over his mouth so he could not spit it out. Eventually, he swallowed the Tasty Tentacle. I watched his eyes glass up. I felt his skin go clammy.

He was confused and unfocused and I picked him up and said, "Your Great God is waiting for you. It hungers for you. Why would you ever wish to be apart?" I spun him around, with him facing the direction from which he came and pushed him down the hill. He tumbled and fell down to the bottom and then picked himself up and headed away from me. He was probably taking my advice and heading to his final meal.

I found an abandoned motel on the side of a ski mountain and discovered supplies set for the season. I ate beef jerky and potato chips. I drank hot cocoa and I waited for the next group to come to me with a chance to eat something good and fresh.

Nothing came. It was months that I was there and saw no one. My beard grew. My ribs began to show. I was no longer a delicious morsel. Perhaps I was spared due to malnutrition.

By Spring, the supplies had dwindled. I moved on once more. A young family was driving a beat up old car and let me drive with them. I told them that I will not eat with them and I do not want them to eat near me. They thought I was strange but agreed.

We made it to the Canadian border, which was completely unguarded

We parted ways and I wandered Southern Canada, eating whatever I could find, though that was getting harder and harder. I was just a shell at this point.

I would go weeks without seeing anyone. Everyone was eaten or gathered by the piers that their Great God preferred for his feasts.

Some of the encounters I had led to attacking each other for our supplies. Most of the time, I would see another human that was not under the sway of the Great God Grabble or by the delights of fast food cuisine and we would nod respectfully to each other and go about our attempts to survive.

I was not captured for three years. I was getting too hungry and tired to be elusive. The trackers found me easily, so it seemed, and I gave myself up because I had no more fight or flight within me. I was just a silhouette of surrender.

They put me in a train car and we went to the Jersey shore. I should say I was not put in a cattle car. There was so few of us remaining, that they gave us regular coach class seats on the train. And they gave us food and water. Not too much, but enough to continue living until we were fed to an overeating god.

We ended up in the broken skeleton of fun that was Atlantic City. It was a place where people gambled and drank and thought they were having a good time. I was under no illusion./ For I saw in the water, the giant shape of the Great God Grabble/ I didn't not look long at him because I knew I would go mad if I did. No one had to inform me of this. I felt the madness approach just by glancing at it.

I waited in a long line of the survivors. We were given a number and when it was called, we were told to politely offer our body to the Great God Grabble. There was nothing to fight over and complain about. This was what was going to occur. We were going to calmly walk to our death in the mouth of a monster we knew not to look at.

After about half a day of slowly waiting for my number to be called, I notice the day getting suddenly dark. The cloud had formed and coalesced into a barrier from the sun. The followers of the Great God Gabble seemed worried. They kept on stealing glances at the clouds and talking amongst themselves.

Their solution was to speed up the process. They just began to shove us in line into the Great God Grabble's mouth. I was being pushed close and I knew my time was soon.

Then, from the clouds, winged angels came down and surrounded the Great God Grabble like they were angry pigeons.

The angels flew in and out of the god's tentacles and it seemed quite upset about the whole thing. I heard one angel proclaim, "Though our God is not old, we will not give up the world to a senior citizen such as yourself. Please surrender or face consequences that you could not imagine.

More angels appeared and started swarming around him. Now they were less like pigeons and more like bees. And though I am not certain, I think they were stinging the old god. He was swatting at them and howling in annoyance.

Then a hand came from the clouds. It was not a beautiful hand that you would expect. It was not well manicured. The skin was cracked and the immense size of it made us move back.

The hand grasped the Great God Grabble who tore at the fingers, making them bleed. Blood dripped down on us. A drop fell on the man beside me and he drowned right there in the holy hemoglobin.

There was a great battle between the arm from the heavens and the fish god. The hand brought the Great God Grabble up to the sky and the clouds dissipated.

Some time later, we discovered the final outcome of the great battle. The body of the Great God Grabble tumbled to earth. It was soon followed by the body that housed the arm. That God fell to and flattened most of the buildings and hotels of Atlantic City.,

We were now down two Gods. But that was okay, there was so few of us to pray to them.

But that was not the end of the carnage. The carnage does not end with the death of Gods. That would be too easy.

Giant bugs began to pour out of the mouth of the Great God Grabble. The other god, the one with the white beard did not exude anything from his mouth, so that was a plus for that deity.

The Giant bugs must have lived in the belly of the old god and now that its host had gone cold and still, they fled looking for a warm host to nestle in. They looked to us humans gaping about the pier.

They flew to the mouths of the humans and lodged in their throats. Eventually, they burst out of the throat and tried again in another mouth.

People were being killed all around me and it was only luck and the strange odds I had that allowed me to not be a target. The thousands of giant evil old god bugs just missed me. I was the statistical anomaly.

The bugs spread out across the globe and killed a lot of people trying to find a nice belly to settle in. That was what killed the world. The bugs inside the stomach of the Great God Grabble. The other god just stunk up the place as it decomposed.

The bugs stopped flying about a few weeks later. Maybe they could not survive long outside the body of such a large and imposing host. It did a good job with the remaining population, but it was not made to last. There were survivors. There were people who did not die at the hands of the bugs, which I know do not have hands.

I went out of there and gathered as much food as I could. I found a food truck and traveled to the midwest. It was not a Tasty Tentacle food truck. It was one of the imitators that sprung up when Tasty Tentacle started becoming popular. It was a Succulent Squid truck. Yes, even the name was an also ran.

I drove around, gathering up food and water and I slept in the truck. It smelled of second rate seafood, but it seemed that the world now had that fetid odor.

I stumbled across other survivors. We traveled out West to where we are now. I do not understand it, but many of our small band wanted to come here to be close to the water. To the ocean and to things that slept under it. They felt that after all they survived, it was best to be close to the water. So if any other Gods awaken, they will be close by and not have to suffer.

I was of a different mind. I wanted to suffer. I wanted to continue even if I had to just barely make it and burn and break and feel half dead. Half dead means that you are also half alive and I wanted to keep that sensation burning in my breast. I wanted to feel like there was still a spark in me that would not perish. Of course that is so much bunk, but the notion kept me going through these broken years.

There are not enough of us to make a society again. I think we want to build society once more, but I am in no hurry. This time of anguish and desolation is so much more preferred than food trucks and doom.

And what became of the food truck that took me across half the country? What became of the Succulent Squid truck? No one knows. It was rotting away in a nearby field for years and then one day, it was gone. No one could have driven it. It was only a shell at this point. No one could possibly make it get up and move. But it is not there. It has been removed from the story.

I worry about one day seeing someone drive up in a refurbished version of it offering food that will change us, make us different, fill our bellies with dread and butter.

9

Leaving the Story

Little Monster applauded slowly.

The old man heard this and frowned. "In the old time, a mean spirited response like that was called a slow clap."

"Why must you give labels to things that do not need it, old man," Little Monster asked. "Isn't it obvious that I am mocking me? Do I need special names to explain that I have no respect for you or your ridiculous stories?"

Loopy looked at the other, "But you have said before that you believe the stories the old man has told us. You said you believed all of them."

"Yes, I believe them," Little Monster said. "I believe every single one of them and then I hate myself for believing them and that makes me hate the Grayling even more."

One Ear leaned in to what he was hearing, "That makes no sense."

Little Monster jumped up and down, "And his story did? Did you listen to it? Did you understand one bit of it?"

Loopy said, "I was confused about some of it. What is fast food? Is that like a rat you are chasing for the tribe's meal and cannot catch. That's food that is fast. But the fast food you talk about is caught in a truck and the people buy it in a window."

The old man chuckled, "Out of all the things I said and described, that is the part that makes no sense?"

One Ear said, "I liked all of it. I didn't know who the two big people were who fell and crushed the city. Were they anyone we should know?"

The old man thought about it and said, "No. There is no one you need to know."

Loopy said, "I liked this death of the world. It made me hungry though and that never is a good thing. Now we will have to improve as hunter gatherers. We really are not that good at it."

The old man raised his hands and showed that he had been working on the grass plaiting. They were now grass lassos. "You can catch your prey with these," he said.

They boys took the grass lassos and practiced by trying to encircle each other's hands. Little Monster took to it immediately, to no one's surprise.

The old man waved at the boys, "Now go. Use an old craft to catch new beasts. The tribe is hungry. I am hungry. Get us some grub and let's not worry about how the World died. Let's just worry about how we are going to eat tonight. There are no food trucks anymore."

The boys ran off, though Loopy stopped and turned around. He shouted at the old man, "I still don't understand this fast food thing. Or the food truck." He then ran to catch the others.

10

An Addendum of Various Armageddons

The boys did not find the old man on the beach. They searched for him through the dunes to no success.

The boys did not find the old man by the edge of the forest. They heard the wolves and scattered away, only finding each other an hour later, glad that they were all still alive.

The boys did not find the old man in the grassy field. They did spy a few long strips of plaited grass. They figured that he was close.

He was not.

Going back to the village center, dejected and a little bored, they heard a shout from a hut that was the sound of the Grayling.

They entered the dirty hut and saw the Grayling with another old man. They were hunched over a board that once was bright and gay, now it was ratty and faded.

The other old man turned to look at the boys. He had no hair on his head or face. He displayed a toothless smile. "There are children staring at us. Not that that is a strange activity. To see two old farts such as ourselves in this blasted wasteland of a present tense must be a puzzling anomaly."

Loopy leaned into One Ear's one ear and whispered, "He speaks like the Grayling, but more so. I don't understand a thing he said."

One Ear shrugged, "I guess when you get old and white haired or no haired you lose your good words and start talking in nothing but bad ones that hurt the mouth when making them."

The old man looked up and saw the three young boys and nodded. "You found me for more stories of the way the world died?"

"We thought you could bore us some more," Little Monster said.

"I am sorry that I won't be able to do that today," the old man stated. "An old friend from the trying times after the death of the world has shown up for a visit and we are doing what we of the old world did for entertainment."

The other man cackled and pronounced, "We are playing board games. It was the pinnacle of society, the board game. Some might say that it is the deck of cards and all the games hidden in those 52 slaps of paper. But card games are too easy to cheat on."

The old man laughed, "Oh, like you are not cheating in this game as we speak!"

The other old man looked horrified. "One does not cheat at the saintly game of Candy Land. To cheat at Candy Land is tantamount to lying to god. You just do not do that."

"God is dead," One Ear said. "That is what you told us in the way the world died. You said that the God fell down after a tussle and rotted away."

The newcomer looked at the old man, "You have been telling the children how the world died."

"I might have spun a tale or two," the old man admitted.

"The gods died and the world went with them," the new old man said.

"That is how it happened. At least that is how it happened the last time I told the story. Details flitter about, you know."

"Oh, I do. And look, I have a double purple card and have moved ahead of you who is still stuck in the Molasses Swamp."

The old man shook his head, "And you say you do not cheat."

The new old man smiled, "Of course. How would I cheat such an honest teller of tales? That would be absurd. But to think that I could still stack a candyland card deck with my old arthritic fingers is a lovely compliment."

Little Monster walked forward to the two, "Are you saying that the world did not die the way the Grayling has told us?" He looked smug when asking that.

"I wouldn't say such a thing," the newcomer said. "I just think that it is hard for any one man to know the whole story. Especially when you consider that this the only important story left. Such a responsibility to tell this tale. Of course people will get things wrong."

The old man corrected, "It is not about getting things wrong, it is about getting things more right than other things."

Little Monster went nose to nose with the newcomer, "Who are you bald one? You have no hair. You have no teeth and yet you are here and acting like a person in the real world. Who are you and why are you in our world?"

The new old man smiled gums at the youth, "I am Grabble."

Little Monster moved back. Loopy looked at the man and asked, "Is that a name or a title?"

"Is there a difference, young man? If it is a title, then it is also the word that hangs around you. I am noosed up with that name and if it is my title, then it is."

One Ear began to cry, "I have no idea what is going on right now."

Grabble stood up and embraced One Ear, who did not struggle or mind the invasion of personal space. "I am sorry. I am Grabble and there is nothing I can do about it.:

One Ear broke away and wiped tears on a smeared cheek.

Grabble looked at the boys, "So you were hearing stories of the end of the world. They are fun stories. Would you like to hear another?"

The old man, the Grayling, grumbled, "We haven't finished the game. I am sure I was winning and now you are going to tell stories instead?"

Grabble punched back t o the benches and sat down and began to play the Candland adventure. "I can do both. We have multitudes inside, don't you think. Now. We will have stories. Who shall begin."

Little Monster said, "You. You Grabble. You should tell us how the world died."

Grabble nodded. "Is it okay if I begin," he asked the old man sitting opposite him/

"Of course. I honestly would not mind hearing the story. I have always been curious how we got where we are."

And the Grabble told the story as he continued to dominate the Candyland board with old man grumbling and swearing to himself, hatting to lose as every long time survivor hates.

"I was just a child. I was not old at all when the world died. It started at Christmas time. Christmas was a strange holiday during the cold days of the year when we would cut down a tree and put it in our houses."

"That makes no sense," Little Monster said.

"Wait. It gets more nonsensical. There was a day when we children would come down to see the tree laden with presents and we were made to believe that a fat man in a red coat flew around the world in one night giving presents. It was ridiculous and delicious. The fat man gave all good kids presents."

"How did he know to give presents to only good kids," One Ear asked.

"He didn't. He didn't exist. He was made up. The parents bought the presents and lied to us. And all of us got presents. There was no bad children for one evening of the year. Everyone got presents. And the presents were important to us kids. And for some reason, we always wanted the same present that we heard about and bothered our parents to have the fat man give us this one greatly desired toy.

"This year, the big toy was a Nuclear Powered Ornery Ocelot. That was the toy of the year. The Ornery Ocelot was a character on a kid's program and we all loved him and his catch phrase, "Beat it until you are merengue." Don't ask children. We all loved it and we would say it all the time in the playground. Beat it until you are merengue. That was childhood to me and oh how I wanted that Nuclear Powered Ornery Ocelot where it could climb walls and hid in sofas and read minds. At least, that is what the commercials led us to believe.

"We all wanted it so bad and every parent tried to get it. There were not enough of the toy to go around. There were riots in toy stores as parents tried to get the few boxes of the Ornery Ocelot. That was the start. The death toll was high with the parents who weren't smart enough to go Christmas shopping with their kevlar vests on. They deserved to die.

"Now with so few of the toys present, knockoffs began to proliferate. People made fake Nuclear Powered Ornery Ocelots. They sort of looked like the real thing, and they certainly were nuclear powered, which was helpful. And these knock-offs were purchased by millions of parents and wrapped and placed under the tree that was put in the house. Don't ask children, some traditions just make no mistake.

"The problem with these knockoffs is that they were powered by stolen nuclear technology from the former Soviet Block. They were not stable as we found out. Now I should mention that I didn't get the Ornery Ocelot. My parents were awful people and gave me books and educational materials for Christmas. That saved my life, but I still have not forgiven them for not giving me fun presents.

"It was not even Christmas afternoon when the Ornery Ocelot knock-offs exploded into tiny mushroom clouds. They destroyed a neighborhood here, an apartment building there. But nothing too bad. But the nuclear explosions hit other nuclear powered christmas presents and there was a chain reaction where whole cities blew up into cinders. Most of the world was destroyed and the rest was a devastated nuclear wasteland with just a few of us given boring gifts allowed to continue to exist.

"That fat man in the red suit has a lot to explain for himself," the Grabble said and laughed so much that he began to cough up blood. "I hate when that happens. I have only one lung left, can't afford to lose the other one. So no amusing stories from now on."

Little Monster spat, "That is not a proper story of the world dying. I don't believe it."

"Why not, young squire," the Grabble asked.

"Because it is too eas. Too simple. The world does die because of one mistake. It dies from a series of things."

"What is your story then," the Grabble asked.

Little Monster paused for a second and then said, "There was a movie being made in a far away country. I don't know what a movie is, but they were making one. I don't even know zactly what a movie is either but they was making it and they were not going by half. It was huge and big and very expensive. It cost more money than most countries have ever made. It was a movie with lots of fights and cars crashing. It was set in the time after the world died. Only problem was, the place they was filming it was pretty good looking with green grass and streams and birds in the sky. Can't have a wasteland movie with grass and birds. But movies was magic is what I have been told. They treated the ground to make it look like a nuclear wasteland. They put chemicals in the ground. It killed everything. They made the movie and it was a big hit. And people started making movies just like it because one movie was a hit, they were going to make movies just like it and do the same things to the ground. So there were other countries that had the chemicals put in the ground to give it that great blasted wasteland look. The thing is, the chemicals in the ground didn't leave when the movie people did. It stayed. It poisoned everyone. It spread because poison is a greedy fella and likes to wander. It spread all over. It made it to the streams and the rivers and the oceans and did a job making everything like the movies. The world was a blasted wasteland because that's what the script said. And everyone died and it turned out that people thought they wanted to be in the pictures, but not this kind of picture. They were happy just watching it and not living it. And that's how the world died."

Grabble applauded. "Oh. I like that. That's a good one. But I have a question. How did anyone survive?"

Little Monster shrugged, "Don't know. I guess there were some people who didn't like movies. If you don't believe in the movies, you ain't going to die like in the movies."

"What's a movie?" Loopy asked.

"How should I know?" Little Monster shot back.

"I don't think that's the way it happened," Loopy whispered.

"Okay big shot," Little Monster said. "You know how the world didn't die. You tell us all how it did."

Loopy moved back from his cousin. He was afraid of the words. He was afraid of all the words he was expected to say.

The old man played his next card in the game and then said, "It is okay, boy. You can tell us or not. There is no pressure."

"But if you have the power to," Grabble said, "then we would love to hear it. It is so important to know the real past. Do you know it?"

Loopy rounded his shoulders and said with as little waver in his voice as he could. "So I guess the world is a piece of rock that goes around the sun. I know that doesn't make sense. That everything should be going around us, but they say that we aren't the center of nothing. And we are a target at that. There are things that just fly around in space and cause problems. One of the things that made a problem was a big rock. Not like the rock that Little Monster likes to wave around and try to scare us."

LIttle Monster shouted, "It does scare you. It is a great and powerful rock and you cower."

"But rocks in space are bigger. Very big. And it came and hit our planet and it killed a lot of people. I don't know know the rock killed a lot of people, but that's the story and the story wants the rock to be a big deal. The planet was pushed around by the big rock, like a bully that is small but still has a good punch. It moved the planet and it got too hot. It was not too close to the sun. Now things were really hot. The closer you are to the sun, the more things heat up. And they heated up and people were getting bad sunburn and they were squinting a lot and not seeing where they were going and a lot of people walked off of cliffs or walked into traffic.

"So the scientists tried to fix the planet and blew up some bombs to put us back where they were. The bombs killed a lot of people, sure but it worked. The planet moved further away from the sun, but too far this time and it was now too cold and folks became icicles and died. The scientists were not done and exploded more bombs and that worked. We were back to the place we were at the beginning. But there were too many bombs and most people died and that is how the world died. It fixed the problem by killing the rest of us."

Grabble nodded, "Very possible. I like how they tried to fix things and just made it worse. That feels like a very human way to kill the Earth."

Loopy shook his head, "The big rock killed the world."

"But the people made it worse," Grabble corrected.

"I guess," Loopy said, "but the big rock sure didn't help."

"And you? Grabble said to One Ear. "How do you think the world died?"

One Ear pretended he did not hear and kept picking his nose. Grabble repeated the question and One Ear said, "Do I have to?"

"No," Grabble admitted, "but it is nice to hear from everyone. And I am sure you know exactly how the world died."

"Yeah," One Ear said softly. "Yeah I think I know how the world died. It didn't."

Little Monster made a raspberry with his lips, "Oh come on, idiot. The world died and that's why we are here like we are."

One Ear said, "No. The world did not die. And this might not be a great life, but this is what the world has always been."

"The world has always been a blasted wasteland, come one!" Little Monster shouted.

"It's not a great story," One Ear admitted, "but there was never a better life. There was never great planes in the sky or large schools or fast food. All of that is bunk. And I don't even know what bunk is, but I know all of that is it."

Grabble smiled and said, "Now that is a story that I kind of like. But what about the Grayling and myself? How could we remember the shining past if there wasn't one?"

One Ear nodded, "Because you are lying."

"Lying," the old man said. "You think we were lying?"

"Of course," One Ear said. "The world has always been this way and you are telling us bunk."

"But why would we do such a thing?" the old man asked.

"I don't know. Maybe you want us to not know things. Maybe you want us to believe there is something better when there really isn't. Maybe you are not old men but something else. Maybe you are always playing games like that with the colors and the candy."

"God and the Devil playing chess?" Grabble asked and laughed. The laughter was harsh, but the old man joined and they laughed long enough that the three boys began to squirm and look around at each other.

Grabble stood up and he was short, shorter than the boys. "That is some story. All of the stories were lovely, but I must be going."

"We haven't finished the game," the old man said.

Grabble looked at his friend, "When have we ever finished any game? It's better to never win or lose. Just to play."

"Of course," the old man said and stood and embraced Grabble. They whispered to each some words that the others were not permitted to hear. Grabble ambled our and was off toward the woods.

"He shouldn't head that way, it's deadly," Loopy whimpered.

"He will be fine," the old man said. He slowly, painfully gathered up the game pieces and the cards and put them and the board in a canvas sack. The old man placed it on a shelf and brought out a deck of cards. "Now boys. Time for stories is over. Who wants to play some cards?"

The boys looked at each other and then back at the old man and sat down and waited for the deal.

About the Book

How did the world die?

It certainly did not survive. It has been many years since things perished. But how?

The young boys want to know. They ask the Grayling, the old man who was there during the time of the death of the world.

He tells the tale. The tale of how the world died. It might have to do with over affectionate rodents. It might have to do with alien invasions or zombies or addictive grinders at a food truck.

There are so many ways that the world might have died. The old man knows them all. The old man doesn't know a damned thing.

The boys listen because the story is large and entertaining. And you will read it to the end, because that's what happens with stories about the death of the world, you can't stop yourself from reading to the end. The end of everything.

Writer's Note

This was written over a few weeks at the end of 2023. I was specifically inspired to write this by my reading "The Scarlet Plague" by Jack London. It is a brief book, though not as short as this one. I took the format for this from his excellent story. His has an old man tell the story of the long ago apocalypse to three grandchildren. The kids are not smart and they certainly do not learn anything from the story they are told by the old man. That book is well written and there are some similarities between the Scarlet Plague and Covid. That's what some readers say, but to me, it is just a good story. And it inspired me to try my hand at something similar. I finished reading the book while on a walk around the neighborhood and when I got home, I began my own version. If you liked my work, you might want to give London's work a shot. He is so much more than Call of the Wild and White Fang. Give him a chance.

About the Writer

David is an author of well over a 100 e-books. They are all kind of short. Some are even shorter than this one. He has written novels, short story collections, pop culture investigations, books on writing, memoirs and a few weird things that don't fit into any category. Those ones are David's favorites. His blog, Gin and Tonics Across Worcester was collected into two books. He ran an e-zine called The Long Weekend Review where the author of the issue could write anything they wanted as long as it was completely written in three days. He also has a zine that he is still writing occasionally called Comic Book Hinterland, that attempts to tell of the odd territories of comic book history in inventive ways. He writes a monthly column called The Library of Disposable Art for Worcester Magazine; the first two years of the columns have been collected into an e-book. For decades, he was an organizer of poetry events in Central Massachusetts. He lives with his family near Worcester, Massachusetts. The front of the book has contact information for him. Get in touch. He ain't scary.

The Short Novels

The Story Cycles

Tales of the Reanimator's Saloon
    And then there are those who live in the back of old paperbacks
    Reynold's Home for Retired Time Travelers
    The Madre and Gander Employment Agency
    Death Rides
    The Devil at Purgatory Chasm
    The Further Adventures of Polly Mint Slab
    Emily and Martha